The Grey Lady and the Strawberry Snatcher

by MOLLY BANG

ALADDIN PAPERBACKS

First Aladdin Paperbacks edition May 1996
Copyright © 1980 by Molly Bang

Aladdin Paperbacks
An imprint of Simon & Schuster
Children's Publishing Division
1230 Avenue of the Americas
New York, NY 10020

Also available in a
Simon & Schuster Books for Young Readers edition

Printed in Hong Kong
10 9 8 7 6 5 4 3 2

The Library of Congress has cataloged
the hardcover edition as follows:

Bang, Molly.
The grey lady and the strawberry snatcher.
Summary: The strawberry snatcher tries to wrest the
strawberries from the grey lady but as he follows her
through shops and woods he discovers some delicious
blackberries instead.
[1. Stories without words.   2. Strawberries—
Fiction] I. Title.
PZ7.B2217Gr 1986   [E]   85-29224
ISBN 0-02-708140-0
ISBN 0-689-80381-8 (Aladdin pbk.)

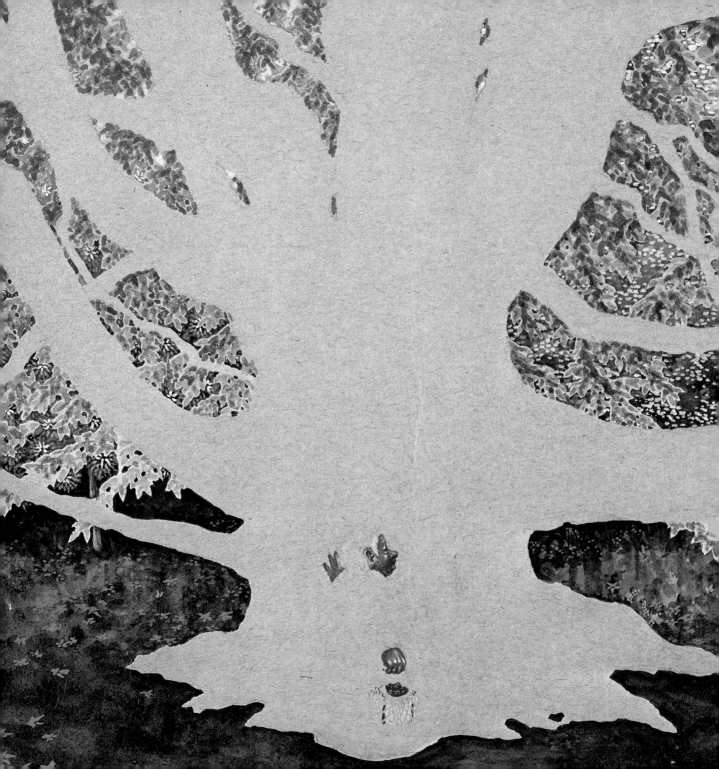

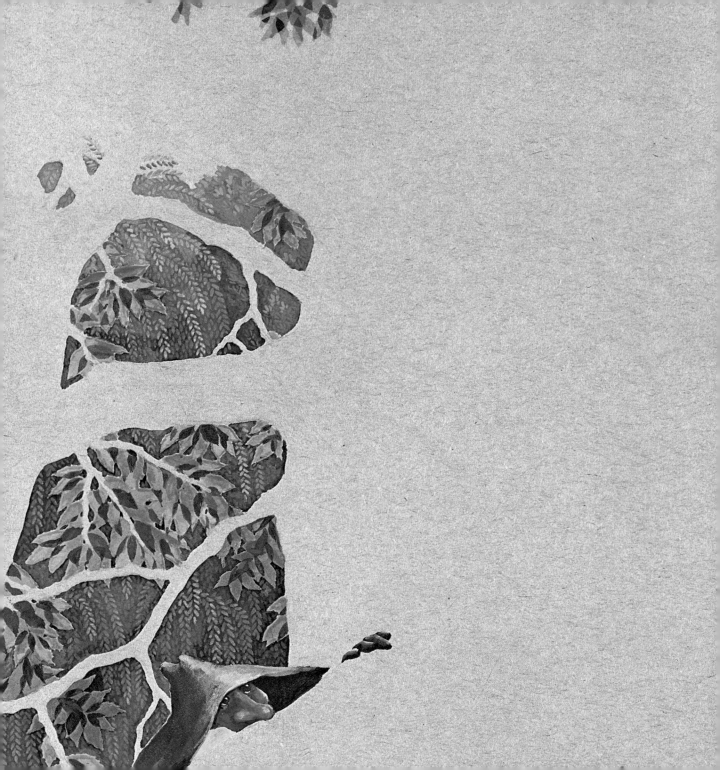

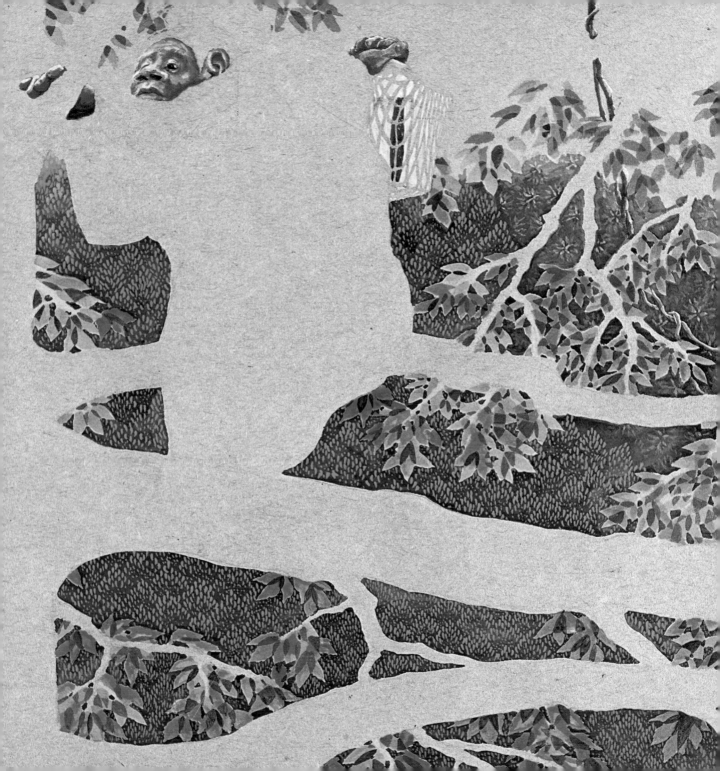

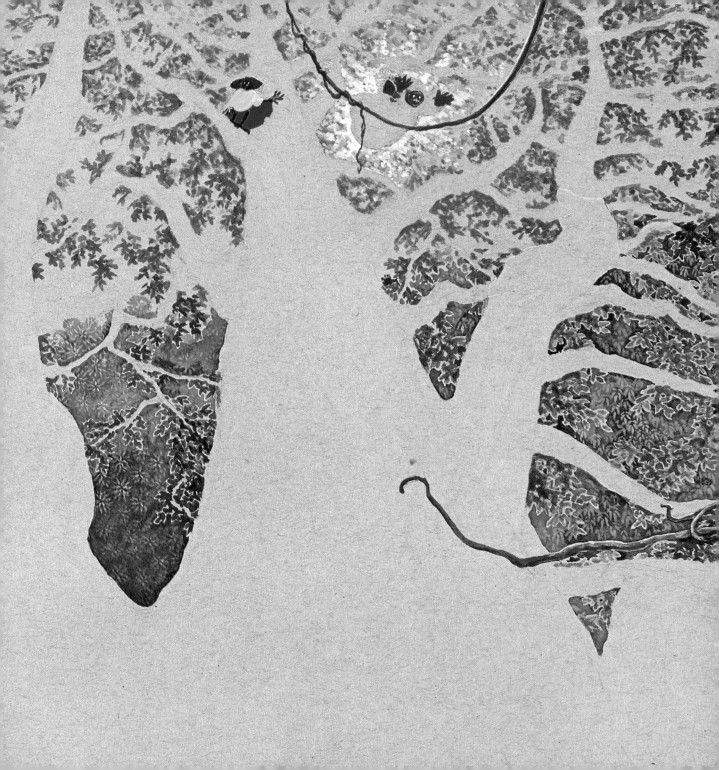